Chapter One

Meet the Wilders

Kids rushing through the crowded house, toasters popping up breakfast, bathroom chaos, backwards shirts, splattered toothpaste, and messy hair. This was just another typical morning in the Wilder household; a house that was built for three, but inhabits six.

"Hurry up! We are going to be late again!" Mrs. Wilder shouted through the house, as her kids ran around grabbing their shoes and backpacks.

Ava Wilder

* Grew up in Hawaii.

* Mom to the Wilder kids.

* Moved to South Padre Island before she had kids.

The family ran out the door, down the long sandy driveway to the car.

"Oh no, my science project," shouted Kai.

"Run back in and grab it. You have ten seconds."

"That would be a lot easier if I had actually remembered to *do* the project," Kai replied through his clenched teeth.

"Kai Wilder! How many times did I remind you to do your homework this weekend?" his mom scolded.

This was nothing new. Kai would miss assignments, but then talk his teacher into letting him make it up in class. He was extremely smart, but didn't think that he had to follow all of the rules.

And why should he? It has been working out for him pretty well so far.

Kai Wilder

* Mischievous

* Smooth Talker

* Caring

"There are only two weeks left of school. We should have a better morning routine by now. Not to mention, have our homework done on time. Hurry and get in the car!" Mrs. Wilder called out.

Just as all the kids were piled into the car, Mrs. Wilder realized that she had forgotten to put her shoes on. "I'll be right back!" she exclaimed as she got back out of the car and ran inside.

When she got back into the car, the kids started teasing her.

"*How many times do we have to tell you not to forget your shoes*?" Coral asked accusingly.

"*Or remind you that you left a curler in your hair*?" Canyon laughed.

"*Oh, or that...*"

"Okay, I get it," Mrs. Wilder cut off Kai as he was about to get in on the fun.

"I may have a little bit to do with why you kids are the way you are, but I wouldn't change a thing about any of you! Is everyone in the car?" Mrs. Wilder asked, as she buckled her seatbelt.

"Nope, we're missing Canyon," Coral reported.

"Awe man, again?" Mrs. Wilder grumbled.

They all looked out the car window just in time to see Canyon, as he prepared to jump off the roof and onto the trampoline below.

"Canyon! What are you doing?" Mrs. Wilder shouted as she rolled down the window.

She wasn't shocked to see that he was on the roof of their house, but she was irritated that he was still not in the car.

He had been the last one to make it to the car all week, and after threatening to take away his skateboard, roller blades, and bike, Mrs. Wilder was sure he wouldn't be last to the car again. Obviously, she was wrong.

"Sorry, mom. A bird's nest fell out of the tree and was lying on the roof. I had to move it back to the tree before the wind knocked it off."

Canyon Wilder

* Twin brother of Coral
* Puts the Wild in Wilder
  (aka the wild child)
* Animal Lover

Mrs. Wilder knew she couldn't be mad at him for that. "Canyon, that heart of yours seems to always get you out of trouble. Now get in the car. If we hurry, we can still make it to school on time."

Canyon crawled over Aspen and Kai and squeezed into the back seat next to Coral.

"Mom, we really need a bigger car!" Coral whined from the back seat, as she was shoving her shoulder into her brother.

"If we could afford a bigger car, we would have a bigger car," Mrs. Wilder scolded, as she sighed.

"I know, I know. It's not what you have, but who you share it with," Coral mumbled.

"Mom. Kai and I talked about it and decided that we are both going to get jobs this summer to help out with some of the bills. Maybe then we will be able to get a bigger car," Aspen offered.

Coral Wilder

* Twin sister to Canyon

* Sneaky

* Super smart

"I appreciate that, but there is nothing wrong with this car. It gets us where we need to go and it's very cozy. I just want you to enjoy your summer. Let me worry about the money," she said with a smile. "Plus, you guys will all be busy at summer camp. Your grandparents would be awfully disappointed if you didn't spend the summer on Menehune Island."

"Camp Menehune doesn't start for a whole month after our summer break. We would have time to do both," Kai said.

"Actually, I have some news I want to share with you, but now is not the time. We will have a family meeting after dinner. We'll go to South Padre Creamery for dessert and discuss our summer plans."

"Can't you tell us *now*?" Canyon asked.

Aspen Wilder

* Oldest of the Wilder kids
* Resourceful
* Leader

"Nope, it's time to go into school," Mrs. Wilder replied as she pulled up to the twin's elementary school.

"Have a wonderful day!" Mrs. Wilder called out the window as the twins were walking in.

Mrs. Wilder pulled away from the drop off line in front of the tall red brick building, and drove towards Kai and Aspen's school.

"I think you two are going to be very excited about what I have to tell you," Mrs. Wilder teased.

"Are you sure you don't want to tell us now?" Kai asked.

"Yes, I'm sure. I want to tell the whole family at the same time."

As they pulled into the parking lot, a group of Kai's friends waited for him to get out.

"Every day, he has a crowd of people waiting for him to get here. I don't get it," Aspen said to her mom, as she got out of the car.

"I guess he's just got that light that makes everyone's day a little brighter. Have a great day, honey, and make sure you enjoy the end of the school year," Mrs. Wilder said as she waved goodbye.

Chapter Two

The Mighty Gator

Back at Coral and Canyon's school Coral hung her backpack on a hook in the back of their large classroom. Desks were lined up in perfect rows from the middle of the classroom all the way to the back. There was a large chalkboard at the front and a huge globe sat on top of the teacher's desk.

The school bell rang. Mrs. Thornhill came in from the hallway and started taking attendance.

"Zach?" she called out.

"Here," he replied.

She continued calling names.

"Dan?"

"Here."

"Matt?"

"Here."

"Coral?"

"Here."

"Canyon?"

Silence.

"*Canyon*?" she repeated.

Silence again.

"Is Canyon sick today?" Mrs. Thornhill asked Coral.

"No. He was dropped off with me this morning and I just saw him at his locker on my way in the…" Coral's voice trailed off as she saw something moving in the tree outside their second story classroom's window.

"What's wrong dear?" Mrs. Thornhill asked.

"Uh, nothing. I'm just not sure where he could be," Coral said shrugging her shoulders and looking out of the window from the corner of her eye.

"Class, open your geography books to page 132 and read through that chapter until I return. I have to locate Canyon," Mrs. Thornhill said in a panicked voice.

Mrs. Thornhill walked out of the classroom and down the colorful hallway, towards the office. As soon as the door shut behind her, Coral ran over to the window and slid it open.

"Canyon! What are you doing?" Coral yelled out the window.

"There was an egg on the ground and I was gonna climb up this tree and look for the nest it fell from. Turns out it's not a

Camp Menehune   18

bird's egg," he said, with a proud smirk on his face. He held it up for Coral and the rest of his classmates to see.

"What?" Coral gasped as she leaned out the window and looked down at the lush green grass, thirty feet below. Staring back at her was a wide-eyed, sharp-toothed *alligator*.

Alligator sightings in South Padre were common, but alligators on school property were *very* rare.

All of the kids were gathered around the window, watching as Canyon dangled over the angry alligator, clasping tightly onto her egg.

CRACK! The branch he was sitting on wasn't going to hold him much longer.

"Canyon, toss me the egg!" Coral yelled. The kids all backed up so that Coral had room around her.

"Toss it on the count of three. One, two, three!"

Canyon gently tossed the egg toward the window. Coral reached out and snatched it from the air, then wrapped it in her shirt.

"Hold on Canyon," she yelled as she ran toward the door.

"Where's she goin'?" Canyon yelled to the class.

Pretty soon he saw her in the courtyard below.

"Coral, no!"

She had picked up a shovel somewhere along her way outside, and was slowly moving toward the alligator.

When she was about five feet away, Coral put the egg on the shovel and held it out towards the alligator. Then she gently lowered the shovel to the ground. The egg rolled off and landed right next to the green giant.

Coral backed away slowly and then turned and darted into the school. The alligator grabbed the egg in her long snout and crawled away. As soon as the alligator was out of sight, Canyon started climbing down the tree. He stretched his leg out to the branch beneath him.

When his foot hit the branch below, the stick he was holding onto, broke off completely, putting all of his weight on one tiny limb. Within seconds, that branch broke off too. He jumped over to the classroom window and was hanging onto the ledge. A couple kids grabbed onto his arms and pulled him through the window as they all went tumbling on the floor.

As the kids were cheering and patting Canyon on the back, Mrs. Thornhill stormed back into the room, "Why is everyone out of their seats?" she snapped.

Coral snuck in behind her and slid into her chair, without Mrs. Thornhill noticing.

"Find your seats and get out your pencils. We are going to take a quiz on the pages you were supposed to be reading. Canyon! Where did you come from? I searched the whole school, and just left your mother a very frantic message."

"I wasn't feeling well. I had to unleash the brown bear... If ya know what I mean."

"No, young man. I do not know what you mean."

"I had to download a brown-load," he said while raising one eyebrow at her.

"Canyon Wilder, when your mother calls me back, she and I are going to have a long chat," Mrs. Thornhill scolded.

The kids in the class laughed hysterically as they prepared to take a quiz, which they definitely weren't ready for.

Over at Water's Edge Middle School, kids were rushing to their second hour classes. Aspen knew that if she stood in the courtyard, she would be able to reach the largest number of people passing by. She had a stack full of flyers and a heart full of hope. If she could recruit just 50 people to pick up trash on the beach after school, they could get the whole North end of the island clean by sunset.

Unfortunately, kids were whisking by her (some nearly trampling her) just to make it to class on time. They barely noticed her standing there.

"Kai! Over here!" Aspen shouted at her brother as he cruised through the courtyard on his skateboard.

"Will you help me pass these out?" She asked.

"You got it!" He took the stack of flyers and went up the swirling cement ramp through the courtyard, to the fourth floor. He let out a whistle that could be heard from a block away. Everyone stopped and looked up at Kai, who was now leaning over the railing.

"Everyone who takes one of these flyers and participates in beach clean-up is invited to the after party; bonfire on the beach. Thrown by yours truly. You won't want to miss it!"

And with that, he tossed the flyers in the air. All of the kids were jumping to catch them. Once the courtyard cleared, there was not even one flyer left on the ground. A party thrown by Kai was a party that everyone wanted to be at. He picked up his backpack and rolled off.

"Thanks Kai!" Aspen yelled as she took off towards her next class.

Chapter Four

As Mrs. Wilder pulled into her work parking lot, she noticed a huge crowd scrambling near the entrance of the Sea Turtle Rescue. She jumped out of her car and ran to see what was going on. When she looked up, she saw a pelican stuck in the telephone wires above the building.

She had been begging the city to run the lines underground for years, but they wouldn't listen. She ran inside to the janitor's closet, pulled out the tallest ladder she could find, and ran back outside. She decided that if she put the ladder on the roof and stood on the very top, she would be able to reach the entangled pelican.

She ran up the stairs that led to the roof as her co-workers chased after her.

"Mrs. Wilder! Stop!" they shouted. "We will just call the fire department. You can't go up there."

"We don't have time to call anyone. This pelican has five minutes, at the most. If we don't get him out before that, he'll die." She climbed up the ladder.

"Hold it steady for me!" she yelled down to the bottom of the ladder as a crowd of people surrounded her.

"Ana, no!" she heard a familiar voice shout. It was Max Hayden, the late Mr. Wilder's best friend. "Kale would not approve of this!" he shouted.

Kale Wilder

* Ornithologist
* Father to the Wilder kids.

Passed away after falling from a power pole while saving an entangled pelican.

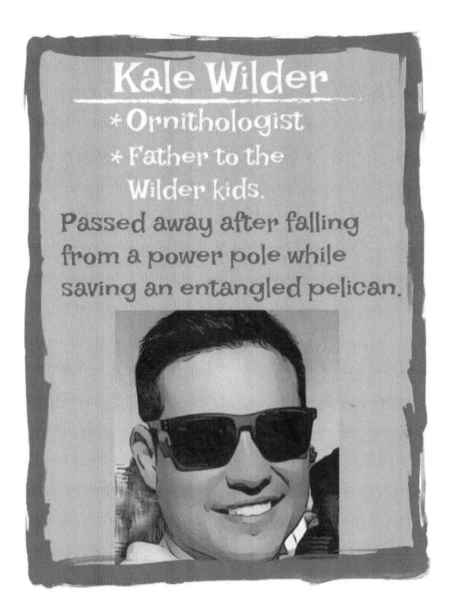

"Max, if Kale were here, he'd be doing the same thing!" she shouted down to the ground as she reached towards the flapping pelican. She started untangling the feisty bird.

"Hold on. I've almost got you," she whispered to the beautiful chestnut colored pelican. Once she freed him from the line, she tucked him under her arm and began descending the ladder.

As she was climbing down the steps, the pelican started flapping and whipping its body from side to side, knocking Mrs. Wilder off of the ladder. As she was falling, the pelican flew out of her arms and was caught by her boss, Finn. Just before Mrs. Wilder was about to hit the ground, Max caught her.

"Whew! Thanks Max. That was a close one."

She brushed some dirt and feathers off of her pants and took the pelican from Finn. The crowd applauded as she took the bird into the building.

After closely examining the pelican, they determined that he sustained no injuries, and were able to release him that same afternoon.

Chapter Five

The Big News

After work, Mrs. Wilder rushed to pick up Coral and Canyon.

"So, what's the news mom?" Canyon asked as soon as he got in the car.

"Not yet," Mrs. Wilder told him, "we have to wait for Aspen and Kai."

"C'mon mom, we've been waiting all day," Coral begged.

Mrs. Wilder stayed silent. As she pulled into her driveway, she saw her mom standing on the porch waiting with Aspen and Kai.

"Kuku!" the twins shouted at the same time. They all jumped out of the car and ran to hug her.

"Mom, what are you doing here?" Mrs. Wilder asked.

"I heard you had some big news to share with the kids tonight, and I wanted to be here for it."

"Kuku, you came all the way from Hawaii, just to hear the big news?" Kai asked.

"I guess that's not the only reason I came this far. I also heard there was going to be *ice cream* involved."

The kids laughed and they all went inside the house. Kai and Aspen took their grandmother's suitcases to their bedroom.

"Wow. Whatever mom is going to tell us, must be pretty important," Aspen said.

"Whatever it is, I hope it's not bad news. You don't think something bad happened, do you?" Kai asked.

"I don't think so. She and Kuku both seem really happy," Aspen responded.

"Aspen, Kai, Canyon, Coral, dinner is ready!" their grandmother shouted from the kitchen.

They all gathered around the kitchen table and had their dinner.

"Kuku, how are Tutu and Camp Menehune?" Aspen asked.

"Your grandfather is great, and Camp is..." Kuku paused, "well that is what we are going to talk about at the creamery."

"Right now, I want to hear about you sweet kids. Canyon, let's start with you. Tell me what's new with you, dear."

"I have only gotten suspended two times this year, and only *one* of those times was my fault."

"What? You told me that they weren't getting in trouble this year," Kuku snapped at Mrs. Wilder.

"I just didn't want you to worry," Mrs. Wilder told her mom. "It hasn't been that bad, just a couple incidents here and there," Mrs. Wilder assured her.

"What about you, Coral?" Kuku asked.

"I've been good. I finally made some friends. Too bad there are only two weeks of school left."

"Why did it take you so long, dear?" Her grandmother asked.

"I'm just different than most girls my age. They like to play with dolls and makeup. I like to pick up trash on the beach and volunteer at the Sea Turtle Rescue. I don't have time to shop and play with Barbies. I like to spend my time doing things that matter."

"Don't get her started, Kuku," Aspen laughed.

"What about you, Aspen?"

"I've been busy. I am the student council president, and I am on the school soccer team, basketball team, swimming team, tennis team, and track team."

"Oh my, you are busy! Kai, are you that busy too?"

"No, not that busy. I play football and my mom made me join a couple school clubs that she said would help me learn life skills. I also volunteer at the Sea Turtle Rescue on Saturdays."

"That's wonderful, Kai. I'm so proud of you. Canyon, we will have to work on your involvement in extracurricular activities."

"Enough with the small talk. Let's go get ice cream!" Coral shouted.

They all got in Kuku's rental van and drove to the South Padre Creamery.

"Okay mom, since you came all the way here from Hawaii, I will let you tell them the big news," Mrs. Wilder said.

"Wait! You already know the news?" Canyon asked his grandmother.

Kuku smiled. "Well, as you all know, your grandfather and I are getting older and the camp is a lot of work. We want to retire, but we could never sell Camp Menehune to strangers, so we have decided to give it to your family. This means you are all going to have to move to Hawaii. However, if any of you do not want to move, you need to tell us now, because even if one person disagrees with this decision, you will stay here and we will close the camp."

Mrs. Wilder explained, "This is a big decision, and I know some of you might be scared."

"Are you kidding? This is a dream come true!" Aspen shouted with pure excitement.

"Let's take an official vote", said Mrs. Wilder. "Raise your hand if you want to move to Hawaii with Kuku and Tutu, and run Camp Menehune."

Aspen, Kai, and Canyon's arms shot up in the air without hesitation. But Coral just sat there.

"Coral, raise your hand!" Canyon snapped at her.

"I really love Camp Menehune, but I am just starting to fit in here. Please don't make me leave," Coral pleaded.

"Coral, what about all of your friends at camp?" Aspen asked.

"If we don't do this, Kuku and Tutu will have to close camp forever. You would never be able to visit Camp Menehune again," Kai explained to her.

"Never again?" Coral asked.

"Nope, never again!" Kai replied.

"Okay, I'll do it. Let's move," Coral agreed.

The kids all shouted with excitement. They could not wait to move to Hawaii.

Chapter Six

Moving to Hawaii

As the Wilder family pulled up to the camp, they were all surprisingly quiet. They looked around the camp. It used to be filled with bright vibrant colors and lively greenery throughout. Now the cabins, mess hall, and surf shack were all greyish-brown. Where there were once multicolored hibiscus flowers, there were now piles of black stems and dirt.

"What happened here?" Canyon asked in a disgusted tone. Kai's hand flew across the back seat and smacked Canyon in the arm. "I was just asking. Jeez!"

"Remember how I told you kids that your grandfather and I were getting older?" Kuku began, "we just can't take care of things as quickly as they are deteriorating. Every time we fix one thing, two more things break. There's no way we would be able to get camp ready before summer, without your help."

"We have a lot of work to do!" Canyon said as he looked around with wide eyes.

"Canyon!" All of the Wilder kids yelled at once. Canyon had a tendency to say whatever popped into his mind, even if it sounded rude.

"Just sayin'," Canyon shrugged.

"Tutu!" The kids cheered as they all ran to greet their grandfather at the door of the main house.

"I'm so glad you're here and have accepted our offer. We will start getting this camp in tiptop shape, first thing tomorrow morning. Tonight, let's go have a Hawaiian favorite, chocolate haupia cream pie," Tutu said as he hugged them.

The main house was huge, and every room had a Hawaiian theme. It was a beautiful house and the whole Wilder family agreed that they had been cramped in a tiny house for far too long.

Chapter Seven

Repairing Camp

The next morning, the kids woke up to the smell of eggs, Portuguese sausage, and rice. Their mom and Kuku had filled the long kitchen table with a traditional Hawaiian breakfast.

Kuku greeted them, "We thought you kids might want to fill your bellies before you start working on the camp. Tutu is going to tell you what job you'll each be starting with."

Tutu came in the kitchen and stood at the head of the table, "Coral and Canyon will be in charge of gardening. Start at the entrance and work your way back through camp to the main house. Kai, I heard your mom made you join a construction club at school, so I'm going to put you in charge of nailing up loose boards and painting. This will need done to all of the cabins, the mess hall, and the surf shack. Aspen, I need you to get the inside of the cabins ready. They need new bedding and curtains. Does everyone understand what they need to do?"

"Yes sir!" they all replied.

"Wonderful! Your mom, grandmother, and I will be around to help each of you, as needed. Everyone put your hands in the middle of the circle. On the count of three, we will shout "family" in Hawaiian. Ready?

"'Ekahi, 'elua, 'ekolu... Ohana!"

Everyone headed in the direction of his or her job. The twins started digging and planting, Kai started painting, and Aspen started cleaning and decorating the cabins.

What should have only taken the family one week to complete, ended up taking over three weeks. The cabins all turned out different colors than what the paint cans said they would be. Small cactuses grew instead of the hundreds of hibiscus flowers that the twins had planted.

Every time Aspen would leave a cabin, she would come back to it being locked with no keys in sight. When she *did* find keys, they wouldn't work, almost like the locks had been changed. This happened so often, that they all decided to take the doors off the hinges until the project was complete.

"Wow! I think we are finally done! That took a lot of persistence, but I knew we would wear those Menehune's out," Tutu said.

"*TUTU!*" Kuku scolded.

"The what?" Coral asked.

"Oh, umm, nothing. You kids did great work," Tutu stammered.

"I just built a fire out by the water. You kids go tend to it, and we will bring out hot dogs, and stuff to make s'mores," Kuku said.

Chapter Eight

What's a Menehune?

Kai, Aspen, Canyon, and Coral sat around the campfire waiting for the food to get out there.

"I wonder what Tutu meant when he said we wore out the Menehune," Aspen wondered out loud.

"Yeah what's a Menehune?" Coral asked, again.

"A Menehune is a dwarf who lives deep in the jungles and hidden valleys of the Hawaiian Islands. They are known to be great craftsman, but even better pranksters," Canyon chimed in.

The siblings all looked at Canyon, shocked that he knew that.

"How do you know?" Kai asked him.

"I did a report on them last year, after I told my teacher about Camp Menehune. She wanted to know more about it, so she made the Menehune my report subject," Canyon said. "All these years that you two have been alive and you didn't know what our family's camp name meant?"

"I just figured it was some Hawaiian word that had something to do with camp," Kai said.

"Yeah, I never gave it much thought," Aspen added.

Their grandfather, grandmother, and mother came out to the fire and they made dinner.

"You kids better go to bed early. We have to train the counselors tomorrow, and we all need to get plenty of rest," Tutu said.

They all headed inside the main house and went to bed. Aspen couldn't wait for the other counselors to arrive the next morning. Every one of them was from a different part of the United States, and for nine years in a row, they all came together at Camp Menehune for the summer. She was even more excited this year because she was finally 14, and old enough to be a camp counselor.

Chapter Nine

Welcome to Camp!

The counselors arrived at Camp Menehune at eight o'clock the next morning. Once camp started, they were each assigned a cabin that they would be in charge of; each cabin housing three or four kids.

The counselors finished training and put away their things. That night on the beach, they played volleyball and had a bonfire with Aspen and Kai.

As the night was coming to an end, the kids gathered around the campfire for scary stories.

"Once upon a time, a long time ago, campers were disappearing from their cabins in the middle of the night," Kai began. "They would hear large footsteps and when they would get out of bed and look out of their windows, **SWIPE**! The Nawao Giants would reach their hands in and snatch the kids. Once they had the kids, they would..."

"KAI WILDER! I have told you before NOT to talk about the Nawao Giants," Tutu interrupted. "It's time for bed kids. We have an exciting day tomorrow and we all need to get some sleep."

"Welcome to Camp!" Mrs. Wilder's voice carried through the courtyard as the buses pulled up to the entrance of the camp.

The kids poured out, one by one. Everyone was smiling, eager to start their summer with their Hawaiian camp family. Camp counselors in colorful shirts helped direct the kids to their cabins.

Aspen raised her hand and shouted to the crowd of campers, "Sydney, Kylie, and Sage, you will be joining me in the Manatee cabin!"

Next up was the Shark cabin. These were the twelve-year-old boys. Daxton stood up on a big rock and called out, "Oliver, Kai, Barry, and Everette! Follow me to the Shark cabin!"

The boys followed Daxton.

"Oliver and Kai, good to see you again. You two must be Barry and Everette," Daxton said as he turned to the two unfamiliar campers. "I'm Daxton, but you can call me 'The Beast'!"

Barry and Everette just stared at him, intimidated.

"Don't listen to him," Kai said, "I can give you a list of things to call him, and *'The Beast'* is not one of them."

"Okay, okay. I see how this summer is going to go," Daxton chuckled, "In all seriousness, you can call me Dax. I will be your counselor for the summer."

Suddenly they heard a high pitched cheer coming from the North side of the courtyard, "D-O-L-P-H-I-N-S! We are proud to be Dolphins! YES! YES! YES! If your name is Ember, Avery, or Paris, follow us this way. We get to decorate our cabins today, today, today!"

It was Kendall and Lola. They were best friends and inseparable, so they decided to be co-counselors for the Dolphins .

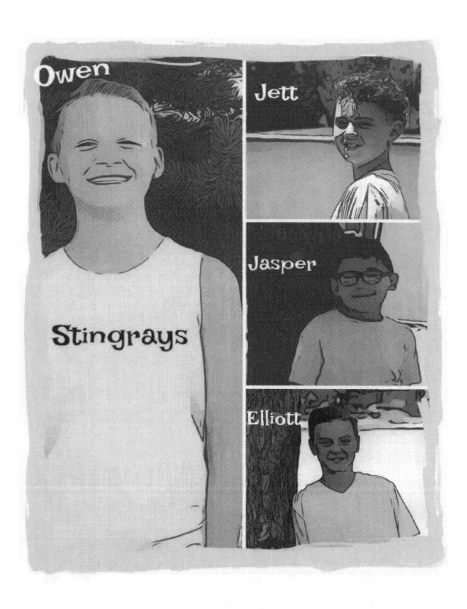

"Yo little surfer dudes!" Owen shouted while standing on top of the bus. Nobody was quite sure when or how he climbed up there, but he was always doing things out of the ordinary so no one gave it a second thought.

"I'm your counsel dude, Owen. If your name is Jett, Jasper, or Elliott, meet me at the Stingray's homestead."

"Next up we have the Whales. Coral, Daisy, and Mac you're with me," Raven told them. This group was a little different from the rest. Coral and Daisy were eight years old, but Mac was only five. She was Raven's little sister. Because their mom travelled so much for work, the only way Raven could come to Camp Menehune this year, was if she let her tag along. Mac loved hanging out with the older girls and Raven didn't mind the extra company.

"Last, but not least, we have the Turtle cabin!" Ryder shouted out the names of the campers that would be in his group, "Canyon, Jess, and Riley follow me."

Immediately following cabin assignments, Mrs. Wilder's voice boomed over the loud speakers, "Welcome back campers. There are a lot of familiar faces around here and a lot of new faces as well. We will have introductions tonight at eight o'clock around the campfire. Right now, I would like for everyone to get unpacked and check out the camp. We will have dinner in the Mess Hall at six o'clock."

Mrs. Wilder dismissed the campers, and they headed to their cabins to start unpacking.

Chapter Ten

Mess Hall Mayhem

Just as instructed, all of the campers showed up at the Mess Hall for dinner at six o'clock that evening.

Aspen looked across the long room filled with wooden picnic tables, and noticed that all of the campers were just sitting there staring at their food instead of eating it.

"Why isn't anyone eating their food?" Aspen asked Kai.

"I don't know. I went over the menu for the summer and everything looked good to me."

"Mom!" Aspen said as she rushed over to Mrs. Wilder from across the room.

"What's wrong?"

"There's no forks or spoons."

"What? Who was supposed to order them?"

"Me!" Kai said, as he came up behind them, "and I did. I even wrapped them in napkins and set them all out last night."

"Well, what happened to them?" Aspen asked.

"I don't know. They were all here last night. Who else has been in here today?" Kai asked.

"Just the chefs. "I'll go talk to them later, but we have to figure something out in the meantime," Mrs. Wilder said in a panic.

Aspen stood on a table and shouted.

"Hey! Hey! Camp-mates! You're probably wondering where your utensils are. Well, wonder no longer, because we have a crazy dinner game that does not involve forks or spoons. How are you going to eat your mac and cheese, you ask? Well let me tell you. First you need to find a group of five campers," Aspen instructed.

"Oh boy. What is she doing?" Canyon asked Coral.

"I don't know, but she usually has good ideas, so let's just follow her lead," Coral answered.

Aspen continued, "Once you have your group of five, sit at a table with another group of five. Each person in your group will pick an animal, but don't tell anyone what animal you picked. When it is your turn you will begin eating your food, the same way that the animal you picked would. Both teams will go at the same time. The first team to guess the animal that you are acting out, will win that round. Continue until everyone on your team has cleared their plate. Don't worry, we will not eat like this every night. We just thought it would be a good way to bond on the first day and get all the craziness out of your system. On your mark. Get set. Go!"

The campers went crazy. At Coral's table, Daisy was shoving food in the sides of her cheeks. They looked like two big balloons that were about to bust.

"SQUIRREL!" Coral shouted. Daisy held her hand up for a high five to let everyone know that Coral was correct.

Over at Oliver's table, Everette had one end of a straw up his nostril and the other end stuck into a pile of mashed potatoes.

"ANTEATER!" Oliver yelled.

"YES!" Everette shouted with joy.

Across from them was Canyon's team. Jess had his hands tucked under his armpits and was pecking at his plate with his mouth.

"Uhhh. Dog?" Canyon asked.

Jess kept pecking.

"Turtle?" Ryder asked.

Jess slid his legs out from under the table and stood on one foot while continuing to peck at his food. When he went down for one last peck, he lost his balance and went face first into his plate of food.

"Flamingo!" Canyon shouted.

Jess slowly lifted his head off of his tray and smiled.

"Yes!" he said, with a face full of pudding.

After dinner, all of the campers were free to explore the campground until it was time for the introductions around the campfire. Aspen and Ryder sat down at one of the tables in the empty mess hall.

"Wow! That was amazing, Aspen! The way you just pulled through like that. The campers had a blast, and no one knew that wasn't the plan all along."

"Thanks Ryder, but what do you think could have happened to all of the utensils?"

"Well, if Kai was the one in charge of ordering them, are we sure that they actually made it here?"

"Kai wouldn't lie about that. If he had forgotten to order them, he would have fessed up. I also don't think the chefs would have had anything to do with it."

Just then, Aspen and Ryder heard yelling coming from the kitchen.

"Who is that?" Ryder whispered.

"It sounds like my grandfather."

"I've never heard Tutu yell," Ryder replied.

They tiptoed over to the kitchen to try and see what was going on. It was Tutu, and he sounded angry. They wondered who he was talking to, and why he was so mad. Most of his words were muffled through the door.

"Is he yelling about the Menehune?" Aspen asked Ryder.

"That's what it sounds like to me," Ryder replied.

The kitchen door swung open, "How long have you been in here? What did you hear?" Tutu asked.

"Nothing sir," Ryder answered.

"Tutu, is something wrong?" Aspen asked.

"No Aspen, I have it under control. Do not worry about it. Go have fun. It's almost time for the bonfire."

Aspen and Ryder exchanged glances and walked out of the mess hall.

"We need to gather all of the Wilder kids and all of the counselors for a meeting after the bonfire. You tell the boys and I'll tell the girls. We can have them meet us on the dock at 10:30. Everyone else should be in bed by then," Aspen said.

Chapter Eleven

Camp Watch

After the bonfire, the counselors walked their groups to their cabins. When everyone was asleep the counselors and the Wilder children headed back to the dock.

"I called you all to this meeting because we had several things happen at camp today with no explanation, like the issue with the missing utensils. I overheard Tutu yelling about the Menehune. This is the second time he has mentioned them, and I don't think it's just something that we can ignore.

"So you think the Menehune are real?" Coral asked, with a concerned look on her face.

"I'm not sure, but I need everyone to be on the lookout. I want you watching for anything strange going on around you. If we're all alert, I'm sure we can figure out what is going on. Take notes about any problems that occur during the day. Let's meet here again tomorrow after everyone has gone to sleep and go over all of our notes," Aspen instructed.

"Kai probably just forgot to put in the order," Canyon said.

"I did not forget!"

"Well I wouldn't be surprised if you did," Coral chimed in.

"Canyon and Coral stop arguing! If you're not going to be helpful, you don't have to come to the meeting tomorrow," Aspen scolded. "I think we should take shifts overnight for the next three days. We can split up into pairs and each take a two-hour shift."

Kai announced the pairs and the shifts they would be taking. Starting off the night from eleven o'clock to one o'clock would be Aspen and Ryder. Aspen had a feeling that Kai did that on purpose, but she wasn't going to complain. Aspen had had a crush on Ryder since they were five years old.

All of the other kids went to their cabins and set their alarms for their assigned time. Ryder looked at Aspen, "Why would someone steal all of the forks? I'm sure they are trying to mess up camp, but why?"

Aspen shrugged. She and Ryder continued to sit there and talk for the rest of their two hours waiting for something suspicious.

"I'm glad you guys decided to take over Camp Menehune. I don't know how I else I would have spent my summer. There really isn't a better way to spend my time than with you, um... and all of our other camp family," Ryder stammered.

Aspen could feel her cheeks turning bright red. Just then, they heard something rustling through the leaves. Their eyes widened and they looked at each other, then looked back towards the bushes where the noise was coming from.

Could this be what they were waiting for? Could this be the Menehune? What if it was? They didn't have a plan, Aspen thought to herself. The bushes continued to rustle. It was getting louder and louder.

"Hey!" Kai laughed as he stumbled

through the bushes with Oliver, "our turn!"

"Kai! Maybe a little warning before you come busting through the bushes!" Aspen yelled.

"Sorry, I tripped. You guys see anything unusual?" Oliver asked.

"You mean besides you guys? Nope. Nothing," Aspen said, a little irritated.

"Hey Aspen, if you're not tired, you can take Kai's shift and hang out with me," Oliver suggested.

"Uh, no thanks. See you tomorrow."

Three days went by and nothing happened. No missing utensils. No vandalism. Nothing.

The kids were getting tired. They wanted to get a full night of sleep, so they decided to stop with the overnight watch and hope that nothing else went wrong during their stay at camp.

Chapter Twelve

Zip-Lining

"Good morning Sharks!" Daxton said as he entered their cabin bright and early, "today we are going zip-lining."

The campers grabbed their things, and hiked to the ladder that led to the zip-line course.

Daxton strapped Kai in and gave him a boost. As Kai was zipping through the Hawaiian jungle, he started looking around.

"This isn't the route we hung the zip-line. There should have been a pit stop by now," Kai thought. He began to slow down, until he eventually stopped completely. Kai hung there for 10 minutes waiting for someone to realize he hadn't made it to the second platform. The plan in place was that when the campers reached the second platform, they were supposed to use the walkie-talkies to report back to the counselor that they made it safely. Once they heard from the previous zip-liner, the counselor would go ahead and send the next person in line.

THUMP! Kai felt a jolt and looked behind him. It was Oliver. He had crashed into the back of him.

"Dude, what happened?" Oliver asked.

"Someone took apart the zip-line route that Tutu and I built and somehow redirected it. Now, I don't know where we are, and our bungee cords are locked, so we can't move backwards."

"I'm sure Daxton will come to help, once he realizes how long it's been since he pushed us out."

They hung and waited, dangling over the Hawaiian jungle. Pretty soon, there was another thump, followed by another jolt. It was Everette, slamming into the back of Oliver, which sent Oliver crashing into Kai, again.

"What are you doing here?" Kai yelled.

"Trying to zip-line. Why are you hanging here?" Everette asked.

Kai explained what had happened, and as soon as he finished telling Everette what was happening, Barry rammed into the back of the bunch.

"Seriously?" yelled Kai. "Where is Daxton? He shouldn't have even sent a second zip-liner until he heard from the first one through the walkie-talkie."

"Oh, he had a new set of instructions pinned to the pole," said Barry.

"What? There weren't any new instructions," Kai said.

"Yeah, they said that the walkie-talkies were broken, so counselors were supposed to wait about ten minutes before pushing out another camper. He said he would meet us at the end to unhook us," Barry told them.

"Great!" Oliver muttered sarcastically.

"How long do you think it will take him to figure out we are stuck out here?" Everette asked.

Meanwhile back at the first platform...

Daxton climbed down the ladder and took the four-wheeler through the jungle to the platform at the end of the zip-line course.

He climbed up the ladder, but when he didn't see any of the kids that he was there to unstrap, he panicked. He climbed down and sped back through the forest to the first platform. He climbed back up, strapped on his harness, and pushed himself off. He zoomed through the air and slammed into the back of Barry, who then slammed into Everette, then onto Oliver, who once again slammed into Kai.

"Why are you all hanging here? I was worried sick about you!" he shouted.

"Daxton, the new set of rules you got this morning were fake," Kai told him.

"The line that Tutu and I hung was re-routed. We don't know where we're at."

"Keep your cool, we will just slide backwards," Daxton suggested.

"We already tried that, but our bungee cords are locked," Kai shot back angrily.

"I have the key in my pocket to unlock the cords, but I will have to unbuckle myself to get it out," said Daxton.

"No!" Kai shouted, "There has to be a better idea."

Before anyone could say another word, Daxton had unbuckled himself and was hanging onto the zip-line with one arm, while pulling the key out of his pocket with the other. He unlocked his harness and was about to buckle himself back in, when his hand slipped. He tried to grab the harness with his other hand, but instead turned upside-down, dangling by his shoelaces.

"Daxton!" The campers screamed.

Barry started swinging himself back and forth to try and get close enough to touch Daxton.

"Grab onto me Dax!" Barry shouted.

"Barry, just take the key, so I don't drop it."

As Daxton reached out to hand Barry the key, Barry grabbed onto Daxton's wrists, pulling him to an upright position. Daxton reached up, grabbed onto his harness, and buckled himself back in. Barry unlocked his harness and passed the key down the line, so that everyone else could do the same.

As soon as they were all unlocked, they slid themselves backwards until they were back where they began.

"Is everybody okay?" Daxton asked.

Everyone was fine, just a little stressed.

"I'm going to talk to Tutu. Everyone else can relax the rest of the afternoon," Kai said.

Oliver, Everette, and Barry went back to their cabin while Daxton, went to find the other counselors to let them know what had happened.

Chapter Thirteen

Boys VS Girls

Back in the Shark cabin, the boys discussed their latest unplanned adventure.

"I think the girls in the Manatee cabin had something to do with the zip lines being messed up," Kai said.

"I was thinking the same thing," Oliver agreed.

"What are we going to do about it? No one will believe that the *sweet* girls had anything to do with sabotaging the zip lines," Barry said.

"Then I guess we need to take matters into our own hands. After the girls go to sleep, we will sneak into their cabin and silly string the whole place," Barry suggested.

"That is the lamest revenge I have ever heard of," Kai replied.

"Well, do you have any better ideas?" Oliver asked.

"Not right now, so I guess we will start with that."

"I don't think that's such a good idea," Everette chimed in, "we don't know it was the girls. What if we get caught?"

"I'm sure it was the Manatees. They have been acting strange ever since they found out about the surf competition coming up. Sydney thinks she can beat me, but she is so wrong. She probably thinks that messing with my mind will throw me off in the competition," Kai said.

"I don't know abo-," Everette was cut off.

"Here ya go boys!" Barry said as he pulled out two large backpacks full of silly string. "I knew these would come in handy."

"Holy motherlode of gooey, stringy goodness," Oliver said.

They each packed a small backpack full and waited for nightfall.

The boys kept a watch out for the girls to turn their cabin lights off. An hour after lights out, the boys knew they would all be asleep.

Dressed in all black, Barry, Oliver, Everette, and Kai snuck over to the Manatee cabin. Everette grabbed the door handle.

"It's locked," he whispered nervously, "guess we better just head back. Oh well, we tried."

"We're not giving up that easy," Oliver grunted as he pushed open the girls' window.

"Yes! Let's go!" Barry cheered loudly.

"SHHHHH!" The Sharks shot back at him.

They each slowly crawled through the window into the pitch-black cabin. They couldn't see a thing, so they just started spraying; covering everything, including each other.

As soon as their silly string cans were empty, they snuck out the window and back to their cabins. The boys cleaned themselves up and went to sleep.

As the sun rose, the golden rays shot through the cabin window and Sydney sat straight up in bed, sensing something gooey covering her entire body.

"Oh my gosh!" she screamed as she pulled sticky green wet chunks from her hair, "WHAT IS THIS?"

Sage and Kylie sat up in their beds and looked at Sydney in disgust.

"What happened to you?" Kylie asked.

"Probably the same thing that happened to us," Sage said as she handed a mirror to Kylie.

"AHHHHHH!" Kylie shrieked in horror.

The girls stormed out of their cabin and into the courtyard.

"MRS. WILDER!" Sage yelled. Mrs. Wilder rushed over to see what was wrong.

"Wow. Trying a new hairstyle, girls?" she asked.

"No! Someone broke into our cabin and covered us and our stuff in nasty, sticky, colorful, gooey silly-string," Kylie cried.

"What is that?" Sydney asked as she pointed to the ground.

They all looked over to see a trail of silly string leading to the Shark cabin. The girls started stomping in that direction.

"Whoa, hold on girls. Just because there is a splotchy trail of silly string leading to the Shark cabin, that does not necessarily mean that the Sharks are the ones that silly stringed you," Mrs. Wilder told them.

"Umm...Yeah, it pretty much does," Kylie replied.

"You're right. Good luck getting them back. I'm going to pretend I didn't see a thing," Mrs. Wilder said as she smiled and walked away.

"Good morning girls!" An overly cheerful voice came from the Shark cabin deck. It was Kai. "Looks like you girls woke up on the wrong side of the bed," he laughed.

"It doesn't even look like they woke up on this planet," Everette said.

"Our cabin is gross. Our hair is disgusting. And you are going to stand in front of us and make jokes?" Sydney shrieked.

"Just wait you slimy Sharks. You'd better watch your backs!" Kylie threatened.

Sage pulled a chunk of gooey silly string from her hair and flicked it on Oliver. Without another word, the girls turned around and marched back to their cabin to clean up.

Chapter Fourteen

Boys VS Girls

PART 2

Later that day, the girls met in the mess hall to discuss their plan to get back at the Sharks.

"Okay girls, we need to pl-," **POP!**

Kylie looked at the girls sitting at the table behind her and rolled her eyes, "as I was saying... We need to pla-," **POW!**

Kylie whipped around again, "What is going on back there?" Kylie yelled at the girls behind her. It was Coral and Daisy.

"We're practicing our homemade volcanos for the competition this afternoon," Coral snapped at Kylie.

"That just gave me a great idea!" Sydney said, "Let's collect all of the practice volcanos from around camp, and place them around the boys' cabin. We can set up trip wires around their beds and when they run into them, it will drop the tablets into the volcanos and make them erupt."

"Instead of dropping in one tablet, let's drop in 5," Sage added.

"Hey Coral. Can we have your volcanos when you are done with them?" Kylie asked.

"For a fee," Coral replied.

"What? You're just going to throw them away if we don't take them," Kylie snapped.

"Why should we help you out?" Daisy asked.

"Just yesterday, in the canoe race, you dropped your oars in the water and stole ours," Coral reminded them.

"We did not steal your oars. The Sharks gave them to us. They said they were extra," Sydney replied.

"The Sharks ended up winning the race. They knew we were their biggest competition. It all makes sense now."

"Ohhh, I'm so going to get them," Daisy grumbled.

"Well, we have good news. We can help you get them back, but we need your practice volcanos, and all of the other model volcanos that we can find," Sydney told them.

Without any further discussion, the Manatees and the Whales started collecting all the old volcano models around camp and piling them in the Manatee cabin.

"Thanks Whales. We will come by and get you tonight on our way to the Shark cabin. Make sure you girls get the exploding tablets from the leftover supplies after the competition this afternoon," Sydney instructed Coral and Daisy. The Manatees went back to their cabin and started prepping the volcanos.

"How much of this powder do we need to put in the bottom of each volcano?" Kylie asked as she started pouring heaping scoops of powder into each volcano.

"Just half a scoop. We just want to make a mess, we don't want to blow their windows out," Sydney replied.

Kylie shrugged her shoulders and kept scooping. She filled them up with half a scoop, but she didn't account for the large scoops she had already put in.

At midnight, the Manatees tapped on the Whale cabin windows, "Did you get the tablets?" Sage whispered into their window.

"Yeah, we have them," Coral answered.

"Come over to our cabin so you can help us load the volcanos into the wheelbarrows," Sage told them.

The girls all snuck across the dark beach courtyard, to the Manatee cabin. Sydney, Kylie, Sage, Coral, and Daisy loaded the volcanos into two wheel barrows, and started slowly towards the Shark cabin.

"Who has the tablets?" Sydney asked?

"I do!" Daisy said as she tossed the Ziploc bag through the air, towards Sydney.

"NO!" The other girls whispered as loudly as they could without yelling. The bag was not sealed shut and hundreds of tablets filled the air. They landed on the ground, in the wheelbarrows, and inside some of the volcanos.

Red liquid started bursting out from each of the clay volcanos. A thick fog and an awful smell filled the air.

"Why are they having this reaction?" Coral yelled. They didn't do this at the competition this afternoon.

"I may have put a little too much powder in them," Kylie said through her clinched teeth, as she tried to avoid getting anything in her mouth.

The girls were covered in the fake lava. Sydney and Daisy were still trying to control the spewing, when Aspen came around the corner.

"What is going on here? I literally fell asleep ten minutes ago and *this* happens? Those better not be my girls in the middle of all this smoke," Aspen said to herself.

The fog started to clear and Aspen was shocked to see that it *was* her girls. They were coated in what looked like bright red paint.

"Manatees and Whales, follow me!" Aspen demanded.

They followed behind her as she marched over to the Whale cabin and knocked on the door. Raven opened the door and was standing there with her eyes half shut, hair a mess, and a sleep mask halfway over one eye.

"Huh?" Raven grunted.

"Wake up. We have a problem," Aspen told her.

"Hold on," Raven mumbled, and she shut the door.

Five minutes went by and Aspen knocked again. There was no answer, so she peeked through the open window.

Raven had crawled into her bed and fallen back to sleep.

"RAVEN!" Aspen yelled through the window.

Aspen's loud voice startled Raven. She immediately jumped out of bed and fell out of the window, landing on Aspen.

"Can you girls keep it down? I've got little Shark dudes in here trying to get some shut eye," Daxton hollered.

Aspen looked up and saw Daxton standing on his porch in his surfboard pajama pants, with his hands on his hips.

"Your *little Sharks* are the reason for this whole mess," Sage growled through her pursed lips.

"We didn't do anything. We've been sleeping this whole time," Kai chimed in.

Kai, Oliver, Everette, and Barry were standing behind Daxton on the porch.

It was then that chaos truly erupted. The girls were yelling at the boys, the boys were mocking the girls, and volcano mess was still spilling out everywhere.

"FREEZE!" Aspen yelled through the madness.

Everyone stopped what they were doing and turned towards Aspen.

"Is this how the rest of the summer is going to be? If we can't get along, we all might as well all go home. Did anyone here steal the utensils from the mess hall? Did anyone here reroute the zip lines? Did anyone here silly string the girls while they were sleeping?"

"Well, we may have had something to do with the silly string... But nothing else," Everette admitted.

"Well, *we* didn't have anything to do with any of it," Kylie said as she held tightly to a volcano in each hand.

"Listen, my boys were wrong for silly stringing you girls and I will make sure they get proper punishment for making such a mess, but we can't keep going back and forth with pranks, or it will never end. Let's spread peace, campers, not boogery messes," Daxton said.

"Wow Dax, that was almost a nice speech," Aspen teased. "C'mon girls, let's go get you all cleaned up and back to bed."

Chapter Fifteen

Parasailing

"Rise and shine, Whales!" Aspen said as she entered the cabin, "I have an exciting day planned for us. Today, we are going parasailing."

"Yes! I've been waiting for this day!" shouted Sydney.

The Whales got ready and met Aspen out by the dock. Ryder was going to drive the boat and Aspen was going to strap in the parasailers, release them out, and then reel them back in.

All of the counselors had to pass a training course on the proper procedures, so everyone was sure it would be smooth sailing. Just to be safe, Aspen decided she was going to parasail first and show the girls what to do.

Ryder strapped her in and climbed into the driver's seat of the boat. As the rope was let loose, Aspen was released into the air. She showed the campers what to do and then asked Ryder to pull her back in.

Ryder grabbed the reel and tried to crank Aspen back to the boat, but something was wrong. The crank was stuck, and he couldn't turn it.

"Hold on, Aspen!" Ryder shouted up to her. He grabbed the walkie-talkie.

"Hello. Is anyone there? Aspen is stuck in the air and we need help."

"Help is on the way," Owen told them. Owen and Raven grabbed their parasailing gear, hopped on a jet ski, and jetted out to sea. As Raven was driving, Owen lifted himself into the air. Raven pulled up next to the boat. Owen and Aspen were flying side by side, high in the sky.

"Aspen, you're going to have to get on my back. Once you're on and holding tight, I'm going to have to cut your cord. Then Raven will reel us back in," Owen instructed.

"Are you sure that will work?" Aspen asked.

"Umm, pretty sure," Owen said without sounding very confident.

Aspen reached out her arms, until she could grab onto Owen's back. As soon as she had a good grip, Owen cut the cord and Raven pulled the two of them back in.

Aspen was almost in tears. As soon as they got back to land, Owen helped her out of the water and she threw her arms around his neck.

"Thank you so much Owen. You saved my life."

Ryder was standing by the boat. He felt awful.

"What were you thinking, Ryder? Why didn't you check the cord before you went out?" Owen screamed.

"It wasn't his fault. We both checked it," Aspen said.

"Nothing was wrong with the equipment. We checked it an hour before we went out.

Aspen and Ryder looked at each other and they knew that they were both thinking about the Menehune.

Everyone went back to the cabins.

Knock! Knock! Knock!

"Who is it?" Aspen yelled from her bed.

"It's me, Ryder."

"Come in!"

Ryder opened the door and slowly walked in, "Aspen, I am so sorry!"

"It wasn't your fault. We both checked the equipment, and the cords were fine."

"I should have checked them again," Ryder said as he sat down on one of the beds. He rested his elbows on his knees and laid his head in his hands.

"Ryder, why are you so upset? I'm okay. Owen came out and got me, and everything ended up being okay."

"I like you Aspen, and I want you to know that I wouldn't ever do anything to hurt you."

Aspen walked over to Ryder and put her hand on his shoulder.

"I like you too, and I know you would do anything to keep me safe. I'll never forget that time when we were six years old and I got stung by a jellyfish. You were the first one to the rescue."

"Oh, no. Don't mention that. That is something I *do* want you to forget."

They both laughed, and Aspen gave him a hug.

Chapter Sixteen

Surfs Up

"Good morning dudes and dudettes," Owen's voice came over the camp intercom, "surf lessons starting at one o'clock. The Manatee cabin will be going first. Check the list on the surf shack door for your cabin's surf time."

At one o'clock, the Manatees met at the surf shack. They all grabbed their boards and found Owen out by the water.

"Okay, grommets listen up. Let's get amped. We're going to the impact zone. If the waves are too gnarly, just bail. I don't want anyone surfing Quasimodo style. No shredding today. If you need to slow down, just pearl. I don't need any of you little dudettes getting stuffed. Our mission today is to learn to Ollie. Let's start out on some ankle busters. ***Cowabunga Dudettes!"***

The campers looked at each other; all very confused.

"What did he just say?" Sage asked.

"I have no idea," Sydney replied.

Despite the fact that they couldn't understand Owen's surf lingo, they headed out to catch some waves.

As they were approaching their first wave, Sydney stood up. All of the sudden, Owen heard screaming. He looked up to see pieces of surfboards flying in the air with chunks slamming into Sage and Sydney. Owen swam out and started helping the girls swim back to shore.

When he turned around, he noticed he was missing Sydney.

"**CODE RED! CODE RED!**" Owen yelled as he assisted the other surfers back to shore. He grabbed his floatation device and swam back out. He saw Sydney flailing about. Her leg was still attached to half of the surfboard by the ankle strap, and blood was running down the middle of her forehead.

Just as Owen was almost to her, the surfboard flew up and smashed him in the side of the face, knocking him unconscious.

The other counselors started running into the water, but Sydney and Owen were too far out. It didn't look like they were going to be able to get to them in time.

All of a sudden, Sydney and Owen began moving quickly to shore. It appeared as if they were running beneath the water, but both of them were obviously still unconscious.

"*How is this possible?*" the other campers and counselors wondered, staring in amazement. As Owen and Sydney approached the shore, two small men emerged from the water.

"Menehune!" Aspen whispered in surprise.

Chapter Seventeen

Saved by the Menehunes

All of the campers ran over to Sydney and Owen as the Menehune laid them on the sand. Owen regained consciousness immediately. One of the Menehune gently tilted Sydney's head off of the ground and she started coughing up water.

"Sydney! Are you okay?" Kylie asked.

"Yes, but I wouldn't be if the Menehune hadn't saved me."

It was silent. Everyone turned and looked at the little men.

"We are very sorry that we mess with surf boards. We take things too far with this prank. We don't want anyone hurt. We just want to make you mad."

By this time, all of the campers, counselors, and staff members were gathered around the Menehune and surfers.

"You tampered with our surfboards? What do you mean *this* prank? Have you been messing with other stuff around camp?" Kai asked angrily.

"We stole silverware," one Menehune said.

"We changed direction of zip-line," said another.

"I jammed crank on parasail. That might have been too much."

"Some of your so-called pranks could have really hurt one of us. Maybe even killed one of us. I appreciate you saving Owen and Sydney, but they only needed saving because of what *you* did! What do you want and why are you trying to make our time at camp so miserable?" Kai shouted.

"We don't want injury for anyone, we want land back."

"This is our land," Tutu's voice boomed. "This land has been in my family for hundreds of years."

"Before your family took over, this was Menehune land. We got pushed into forest when Nawao Giants moved in. Now Big Hawaiian giant taking our forest homes, so we want old land back."

"This is our camp, we are not just going to give you the land back," Kai said.

"We know. That's why we try to drive you out. Sorry to put you in danger, but what else can we do? Forest Giants smashing our homes. We have no money to go somewhere else."

"I think I have a solution," Kuku offered, "we have a lot of extra cabins and we a lot of work to do in order for our camp to run smoothly. Bring your families back to Camp Menehune and we can share the land. You can do some work for us, and in return you can live in a cabin and have access to the mess hall, for meals."

"This deal sound fair. I will take back to Menehune tribe and will discuss. We be back with answer tonight."

That evening the Menehune came back.

"Our family say yes. Thank you and we are sorry again for dangerous prank."

Over the next week the Menehune leaders gathered their things in the forest and came back with their families. They were trained to work in all of the different areas of camp. By the end of summer, the Menehune were part of the Wilder family and were forgiven by all of the campers.

Chapter Eighteen

Knock! Knock! Knock!

"Come in," Aspen said through the cabin screen door.

Ryder walked in with a bouquet of wild Hawaiian flowers. Aspens face lit up as a huge smile drew across her face.

"Aspen, even with all of the problems we've experienced at camp, this has been the best summer of my life. I just wanted to come by and ask you if you would go to the Luau with me."

"I would love to go to the Luau with you, Ryder."

That night at the Luau everyone showed up in festive clothing; grass skirts, coconuts, leis, and straw hats. There were rows of tables stacked with fresh pineapple.

Every year at the final Luau, there is a giant pig roasting over an open flame, but Coral made sure that didn't happen this year. Instead, they decided to have a fire going with a giant s'more bar next to it.

Some of the counselors taught the campers how to hula dance, while others played volleyball. Tiki torches lined paths in the sand, and the stars were shining bright. The last night of camp was perfect.

Made in the USA
Lexington, KY
19 November 2018